# Robert
## and the
## World's Worst
## Wristwatch

**Also by Barbara Seuling**

# Robert

## and the
## World's Worst
## Wristwatch

### by Barbara Seuling
### Illustrated by Paul Brewer

A
**LITTLE APPLE**
**PAPERBACK**

SCHOLASTIC INC.
New York  Toronto  London  Auckland  Sydney
Mexico City  New Delhi  Hong Kong  Buenos Aires

ISBN 0-439-44380-6

12  11  10  9  8  7  6  5  4  3  2 1        4  5  6  7  8  9/0

Printed in the U.S.A.                                40
First Scholastic printing, January 2004

To Oliver and Ellis
—B. S.

For Bob Ruddick and Gery Greer
—P. B.

# Contents

# Birthday Boy

It was Robert Dorfman's birthday. He was nine years old. His mom had made his favorite dinner: hamburgers and french fries, smothered in catsup. Now it was time to open his presents.

"Open mine first," said his brother, Charlie, handing him a package the size of a shoe box wrapped in blue-and-yellow-striped paper. Robert tore it open. It was a model tyrannosaurus rex.

"The arms move, and its eyes light up," said Charlie, grinning.

"Thanks!" said Robert. This would be a great addition to his dinosaur collection. Sometimes, Charlie could be really nice.

Robert put it on the floor and turned the switch to ON. The dinosaur started to move.

Huckleberry, Robert's yellow lab, growled and backed away as the dinosaur advanced, step by step, toward him. Cautiously, he approached it again and sniffed its tail. They all laughed.

"Dogs will be dogs," said Mr. Dorfman.

"Open the silver one," said his mom, pointing to another package, wrapped in silver paper with a blue bow stuck on top. Robert shook it, read the tag, then tore it open.

"It's the Star Wars action figure I wanted!" he cried. "Thanks, Mom! Thanks, Dad!"

"You're welcome," said his mom.

"Sure thing, Tiger," said his dad.

There was a card from Grandma Dorfman in Florida with a twenty-dollar bill inside. "Cool," he said.

The last present was from Grandma Judy. Her card said, "This does everything except cook and wash windows." Grandma Judy was funny. It was a wristwatch. The box said it told the time all over the world, showed the year, month and date, and even reminded you of important appointments.

"Wow," he said, putting it on. He would figure out how to set it later.

"Happy birthday to you, Happy birthday to you . . ."

Everyone sang as Robert's mom brought out a birthday cake with ten lighted candles on it, one for each year plus one to grow on. Robert joined in at the end, almost in tune, "Happy birthday to meeeeeee."

"Make a wish, birthday boy," said his mom.

Robert closed his eyes, made a wish, and blew. When he opened his eyes, the candles were still lit. He tried again, taking a bigger breath this time. The candles were still burning. Charlie laughed.

"Yo, Rob, what kind of lungs do you have?"

Robert tried again, but the candles still didn't go out. By now Charlie was laughing

so hard, Robert knew his brother was up
to something.

"They're trick candles!" said Robert.

Charlie acted like he thought that was
the funniest thing he ever saw. His mom and

dad laughed, too. That Charlie! His brother tricked him time and again, and Robert still fell for it every time.

His mom found the regular candles and replaced the trick ones with real ones. As she lit the candles, Robert made a new birthday wish: He wished his brother would stop treating him like a dumb little kid.

# The World's Worst Wristwatch

Two pieces of birthday cake! No wonder Robert felt stuffed. Upstairs, he flopped down on his beanbag chair. Huckleberry lay sleeping beside him. Robert took his new action figure out of its wrapping and played with it. Then he started the dinosaur and watched it go.

Finally, he got to his watch. The instructions were hard to follow and in teeny-tiny print. He couldn't figure out how to set the time.

Robert thumped downstairs.

"Dad?" he asked.

"What is it, Tiger?" asked Mr. Dorfman, looking up from his newspaper.

"I can't set my watch." Robert's dad loved anything to do with numbers, so Robert thought it was a good idea to ask him.

"There's no such word as 'can't,'" he said.

"Huh?"

"Never say 'I can't,'" said his dad, "or you will believe it and then you won't even try."

Uh-oh. This could be one of those times when his dad felt like teaching him something important. His dad was smart and all, but sometimes Robert just wanted a little bit of help, and he got a whole lesson instead.

"Okay," said Robert. He handed his watch to his dad, along with the instructions that came with it.

Mr. Dorfman took the watch and the instructions, but he looked at Robert. "I think you don't believe me," he said.

"I . . . I do," said Robert. He didn't really know what else to say.

"Get the dictionary," said Mr. Dorfman.

Robert wished by now that he had asked his mom to set the watch, instead. If she didn't know how to set the time, she would just say so and be done with it. He went over to the bookcase and pulled out the dictionary. He brought it over to his dad and put it on the coffee table.

"Open it," said his dad. "Look up the word 'can't.'"

Robert did as he was told. He flipped to the c's—candy—cannibal—canoe . . .

"Somebody wrote in this book!" said Robert. There was a black line through the word "can't." He was surprised. His mom told him never ever to write in a book unless it was meant to be written in.

"I did that," said his dad. Robert looked at him like he couldn't believe it. "That's how strongly I believe in what I just said."

Wow. His dad meant business if he wrote in a book. He wondered if his mom knew.

"Dad . . . ?" said Robert.

"Yes, Tiger?"

"Um . . . my watch. Can you make it tell the time?"

His father looked at the watch again and at the instructions. Then he pressed some buttons, made it beep a few times, and handed it back to Robert.

"There you go," he said. "Date and time." That was good enough for Robert. He didn't need to know the rest, like what time it was in Australia. He wanted to leave before his dad thought of something else to teach him.

"Thanks," said Robert.

"You're welcome," said his father, going back to his newspaper.

Mrs. Dorfman came in as Robert was putting the dictionary back on the shelf.

"We got an invitation in the mail today—to cousin Heather's wedding," she said. Robert remembered cousin Heather. She was pretty, with long blond hair, and she once told him he was handsome. Of course, he was only four years old at the time.

"That's nice," said his dad.

"We'll have to get you a suit, Robert," said his mom. "You can wear your new watch and be really spiffy." Robert groaned. Spiffy was a mom word. He hated being spiffy. He hated shopping, and he hated getting dressed up even more. He liked his jeans and his favorite shirt and his comfortable sneakers.

That night, a piercing sound awakened Robert. He jumped out of bed, throwing Huckleberry onto the floor with a bump.

"I'm sorry, Huck. What's that sound?"

He couldn't find his slippers in the dark and padded barefoot toward his desk, bumping into the beanbag chair. Groggy, he turned on his desk lamp, almost knocking it over. There it was—his new wrist watch, beeping away. He pressed one button, then another. He couldn't turn it off. He pressed all the buttons at once. At last it stopped.

Grandma Judy was great. But she had sent him the world's worst wristwatch.

# No Sleep

**R**obert slipped his backpack on and went out the front door. He could hardly lift his feet. His wristwatch had gone off three times in the night, each time waking Robert up. He was tempted once to throw it out the window, but because it was from Grandma Judy, he didn't.

He met up with his best friend, Paul, two blocks away. They lived close enough to the school to walk there instead of taking the school bus.

Robert told Paul about his birthday.

14

"Look." He showed Paul his new watch. "You can program it to tell you the time in China. My grandma Judy sent it to me."

"Neat," said Paul.

Paul handed him a small package. "Happy birthday," he said.

Robert took the package and opened it.

It was a key chain with a dog-shaped piece of plastic attached to it.

"I made it out of Sculpy," Paul told him, "but I painted it myself." The dog was a yellow lab with a pink nose. It looked just like Huckleberry.

"Thanks!" Robert said. He took his house key from around his neck, where he wore it on a string for when his parents weren't home after school. He put it on the key chain. A new watch and his own key chain! Robert was feeling more grown up every minute.

Robert got through the morning without falling asleep. He yawned, but he managed to stay awake. The afternoon was another story. That's when they did math.

Math made Robert want to sleep more than anything. His brain seemed to melt down, especially with word problems.

"What is the answer to problem number seven?" asked Mrs. Bernthal. Robert stared at his book and read the problem again. Mary plays the violin, the flute, and the piano. Tim plays the piano and the drums. Jessica plays the clarinet and the flute. How many different instruments do the children play?

It looked easy, but every time Robert thought he had the answer and wrote it down it looked wrong. He erased it four times. Math problems always seemed like trick questions. They made Robert's neck itch. Are the drums considered an instrument? Do you count the piano twice?

Thank goodness Susanne Lee Rodgers raised her hand before Mrs. Bernthal had to call on someone.

"Susanne Lee?" said Mrs. Bernthal.

"They play five different instruments," said Susanne Lee.

"That's right. Did anyone else get it?"

Brian Hoberman raised his hand, and Emily Asher. Maybe Robert wasn't so dumb. A lot of kids didn't get it.

Robert was happy to hear the bell ring, finally. He dragged himself along, talking to Paul on the way home.

"I'm going to a wedding," he said.

"I went to a wedding once," said Paul.

"What was it like?"

"There was a lot of music and everybody danced."

Robert saw people dance to bands like The Rubber Tires in music videos. They threw their bodies around in twists and shakes.

"What kind of dancing? " asked Robert.

"I don't know," said Paul. "I don't remember a lot. I was little."

Robert kicked a pebble along as he walked. "I know square dancing from what Mrs. Bernthal taught us."

Mrs. Bernthal had been reading to them from *Little House on the Prairie.* They had just read about Laura's Pa playing the fiddle at a square dance, so Mrs. Bernthal taught them how to do it. Robert kicked the pebble into the street.

"Hmm," said Paul. "I don't know if they do square dancing at weddings. You may have to learn a regular dance."

Great. He had to wear a suit and a tie and good shoes. And now he had to learn to dance.

# Mrs. Crabtree

**R**obert walked into the room quietly. The old woman looked like she was asleep in her wheelchair. "Mrs. Santini?" he said softly.

Mrs. Santini's eyes opened. "Oh, hello, Robert," she said. "I was just taking a little catnap. Come in."

Mrs. Bernthal brought the class to Sunset Pines Senior Home every month to visit the residents and help them with small errands. Robert liked Mrs. Santini. He always brought her her favorite candy bar. Mrs. Santini was old. Robert liked hearing her stories about the old days, just like when Grandma Judy visited.

"Let's go out to the lounge," said Mrs. Santini. "There's more room there." Robert wheeled Mrs. Santini down the hall to the lounge. A couple of people were watching TV. Others were talking or napping.

They chose a sunny spot by the window. Robert sat next to Mrs. Santini in an easy chair. Just as he was about to speak, Robert's new watch went off. *Beep beep! Beep beep! Beep beep!* Robert pressed all the buttons but he couldn't stop it.

*Beep beep! Beep beep! Beep beep!*

"What is that noise?" shouted a sharp voice not far from them. An old woman on a nearby sofa waved her cane. "Stop that racket!" she cried. "Stop it!"

"I . . . I'm trying," said Robert, trying to punch all the buttons he could. Finally, it stopped.

"I'm sorry," he said. He looked at Mrs. Santini.

"Don't mind Mrs. Crabtree," said Mrs. Santini in a low voice. She patted Robert's hand. "She's an old grouch who complains about everything. She isn't very happy. She'll be all right in a minute."

Robert felt shaky. He explained about the watch. "My Grandma Judy gave it to me for my birthday," he said. "I haven't figured it out yet."

"There are many things I haven't figured out yet," said Mrs. Santini, laughing. "But you're smart," she went on. "You'll get it, one of these days. So you've had a birthday. How old are you?"

"Nine."

Mrs. Santini said nine was a good age. "That was the year I learned to roller skate," she said. Robert couldn't imagine Mrs. Santini ever being nine, and on roller

skates! He remembered to give Mrs.
Santini the Seven Wonders candy bar she
liked.

"That's funny. It's your birthday and
you bring me candy." Mrs. Santini thanked

him and told him, once again, to keep the change from the dollar she had given him.

"How is that puppy of yours?" asked Mrs. Santini.

"He's great," said Robert, smiling. He showed her the key chain with the Sculpy dog that looked like Huckleberry.

"Maybe you can bring me a photograph of him next time you come," said Mrs. Santini.

A woman was just passing by when she stopped. "Excuse me," she said. "I couldn't help overhearing you. I'm Marla, the Recreation Director. I was just thinking about a new program, bringing pets in to visit. Is your dog well behaved?"

"Yes," Robert said. "I trained him myself."

"Elderly people like animals," said Marla, "but many of them can't take care of pets, so visits are good for them. I should talk to your teacher. Perhaps your class could bring in their pets one day."

"Cool," said Robert. He knew Mrs. Santini would love Huckleberry. But he had to laugh thinking about what Mrs. Crabtree would say when she heard about this.

# Shopping

**R**obert dragged his feet as he walked alongside his mom. He hated shopping for clothes even more than he hated getting his hair cut at Ernesto's Emporium. They stopped in front of Boys Will Be Boys. "Let's go in here, Robert."

Robert hung back while his mom went through racks of suits. She picked out a navy blue one.

"Try this on, Rob," she said. A salesman led them to a dressing room.

As Robert took off his pants, his watch went off again. *Beep beep! Beep beep! Beep beep!* Robert frantically tried to stop it. The salesman came running in as Robert smacked his watch.

"Is there a problem?" asked the salesman.

Robert stood there, in his underwear, unable to speak.

*Beep beep! Beep beep! Beep beep!*

He punched at the buttons. "It's . . . it's . . . okay," he said, sounding lame. His face was getting hot. "It's just my watch."

Robert's mom burst in. "What's wrong?" she asked.

"It's his watch," said the salesman.

*Beep beep! Beep beep! Beep beep!*

Robert grabbed the pants off the hanger and quickly got into them. You never knew who was going to come in next. He put on the jacket and hurried out of the dressing room. The watch was still beeping.

"Let me see," said the salesman. He took Robert's wrist and looked at the watch. He pressed a couple of buttons, and the beeping stopped.

"Thanks," Robert muttered. How did he do that? Robert had pressed all the buttons, and it hadn't stopped for him.

"Don't you look handsome!" said his mom. "You look so grown up, Rob." Robert couldn't care less. He just wanted to go home.

On the way home, Robert sulked in the back seat. This wedding was not turning out to be any fun. First the suit, and now he had to learn to dance. Charlie had told him once he had two left feet. That must mean he didn't dance very well.

If only someone could show him. Susanne Lee Rodgers must know how to

dance—she knew everything. But he couldn't imagine asking Susanne Lee. She made him feel dumb when she helped him. He could ask Kristi Mills, in his class. She took dancing lessons. The thought of asking anyone made his neck itch.

# Two Left Feet

On his class's next visit to Sunset Pines, Robert told Mrs. Santini about the wedding.

"A wedding? That's wonderful!" said Mrs. Santini. "I love weddings."

"Everyone dances at weddings, right?" If anyone knew, Mrs. Santini would. She must have been to a thousand weddings.

"Yes, of course," said Mrs. Santini. "It's wonderful to dance at somebody's wedding. You're there to wish the couple well and to have a good time."

"What if you don't know how?" he asked.

"So you learn," said Mrs. Santini. "It's not so hard."

"I got a book," said Robert, "but I get all mixed up." Robert took a book out of his backpack and showed it to Mrs. Santini.

"Hmm. *You Can Learn to Dance,*" she read.

"It shows where to put your feet with big Xs, but I always forget by the time I go to try it."

"Maybe I can help you," said Mrs. Santini.

Robert wondered how an old woman in a wheelchair could help him, but he didn't say anything.

"Years ago, when I was a girl," said Mrs. Santini, "we learned to dance by making footprints and sticking them to the floor."

"Footprints?" asked Robert.

"Sure. The TV showed us. We watched people dance. Then they showed us foot-prints on the floor marked 1–2–3–4 so you knew where to put your left foot, your right foot, and then your left foot again. All the young people learned to dance that way. Just follow the footprints."

"That's great," said Robert. It sounded like something he could do.

"Don't worry. You'll learn lots of dances in no time."

"Dances? More than one? I already know how to square dance."

Mrs. Santini laughed. "You'll be fine if you just learn the fox trot. But it doesn't hurt to know a waltz. That's elegant."

"Uh-uh," said Robert. "I don't think so. That's for Prince Charming when he dances at the ball with Cinderella."

"You never know," said Mrs. Santini. "Maybe you will be Prince Charming some day."

Robert smiled. Mrs. Santini was nice, and she meant well. But Prince Charming did not have two left feet.

# Footprints

**R**obert drew a footprint and stared at it. Carefully, he cut out around the heel and toes. The big toe was easy, but the little toes were hard. Robert's hand hurt from holding the scissors tight for so long.

"This is going to take forever," he said out loud. Huckleberry, stretched out on Robert's bed, raised his head.

"Something is wrong," Robert said, looking at the footprint. Of course! Robert wasn't going to dance barefoot. He would have shoes on. The footprint didn't need toes! Huckleberry's head went down again.

Robert took off his sneaker and put it on a clean piece of paper. Then he drew around it with a pencil. There. That was better. He cut out a whole bunch of sneaker prints. That was much easier.

He took off his other sneaker and made footprints from that, too. That was to make sure he didn't have two left feet.

He looked up the dance Mrs. Santini told him about. There it was—the fox trot. Using the Xs in the book as a guide, he put footprints down on the floor and marked them 1, 2, 3, 4, 1, 2, 3, 4. When he finished, he stepped on the footprints, one, two, three, four. It worked. He knew where to put his feet.

When he felt he had it, he plopped down on his beanbag chair to rest. Just out of curiosity, he looked up the waltz. Hmm. Maybe he would try it, just for fun. He needed more room to spread out. This dance took three big steps, making big circles— 1, 2, 3, 1, 2, 3.

Robert put his sneakers on and tied the laces. He picked up the footprints he had cut out, a marker, and the book. He went down the stairs, *thump, thump*. Nobody was home, so he marked the footprints and placed them across the living room floor. One, two, three, one, two, three. He was about to put down another footprint when Huckleberry nudged him.

"Hey, Huck. What's up? You want to go out?"

The big yellow dog wagged his whole body at the word "out."

"Okay." Robert put down the footprints and got the leash. "Come on, boy. We'll take a walk around the block."

When he came back, there were footprints going from the front door up the stairs. Robert followed them. At the top

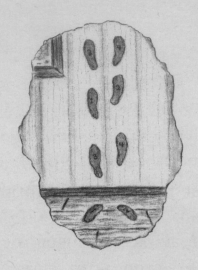

of the stairs, the footprints went straight up the wall!

Charlie came out of his room laughing. "Yo, Rob!" he cried. "Looks like somebody's been here!" He cracked himself up.

"That's not funny!" Robert shouted, pulling footprints off the wall. They had been stuck on with little pieces of rolled-up tape.

"Oh, lighten up, Rob. It is funny!" said Charlie.

"I was doing something important with these," said Robert.

"You can still do it," said Charlie. "No harm done. You take things too seriously."

"What's going on?" called Robert's dad from downstairs. He must have just come home. "What are all these footprints for?"

Robert hated to tattle, but he couldn't help it. As his father came upstairs, Robert told him what had happened. At first, a little smile crept across his dad's face. Then it disappeared.

"Charlie, you have to have more respect for other people's property," he said. He turned to Robert. "Was anything damaged?" he asked.

"No," Robert said. He was glad his father stuck up for him. He picked up all the footprints and went to his room. Maybe he'd never learn to dance.

Robert was doodling his gazillionth footprint in his notebook when there was a knock on his door. His mom came in.

"I heard what happened," she said. "Why didn't you ask me for help?" Robert shrugged. He didn't know his mom knew how to dance.

"Your father and I danced," said his mom. "I was pretty good, if I do say so myself. But your dad had two left feet." Robert perked up.

"Really?" he said.

"Really what? That we danced? Or that your dad had two left feet?"

"Both," said Robert. He laughed.

"Well, you're laughing," said his mom. "That's a good sign. Come on downstairs, and we'll show you something."

Robert and Huckleberry followed her downstairs. They watched as she put on a

CD. She took Robert's dad's hand and started to dance.

They moved this way and that, to the music. "This is the hustle," said Robert's mom. "Everybody danced this in the 70s." Boy. That was a long time ago.

Robert noticed that his dad was a bit clumsy, but his mom kept moving him along. It was great to see his parents in such a good mood. Charlie even came down to watch.

When the music stopped, Robert's mom brushed back some hair that had come loose and changed the CD. This was a bouncier tune.

As the music played, his parents moved to the rhythm. Every now and then they bumped into each other with their hips.

"This one was called the bump," said his mom.

Robert laughed. He couldn't believe how silly his parents looked or that they had ever danced like that.

Afterward, Robert's mom showed him how to do the fox trot to music. At first, it was hard to move his feet without the footprints to guide him, but she made it seem easy.

"Do you know the waltz?" he asked, when they stopped for a rest.

"The waltz? I think so." It took her a while to find a CD to play, but she finally found one.

Robert followed his mom's directions.

"Listen to the music," she said. "And follow my feet. There are three beats. With each one you take another step, making circles as you dance. One, two, three. One, two, three. See?"

They danced around the living room.

First square dancing, now circles. It was like math, but with music—and feet.

With his mom leading, he moved around the room, letting the music sink in. A guy with a deep voice was singing about an impossible dream. Robert listened. Yeah. It was an impossible dream all right. Just look at him dancing!

# Pet Day

The children filed into Sunset Pines. Marla greeted them. "This is so nice of you, boys and girls. The residents are going to enjoy meeting your pets."

Robert held Huckleberry's leash with his left hand. In his right arm he cradled Fuzzy, his tarantula, in a small plastic tank. Vanessa carried a canary in a wire cage, and Brian Hoberman brought his guinea pig in a shoe box. Susanne Lee had Fluffy, her cat, in a carrier. Huckleberry kept sniffing at the little window in the end of the carrier. Fluffy had his eye on the canary.

Marla led the children to the lounge. "May I have your attention, please?" she called. "We have a real treat today. The children from Clover Hill Elementary School have brought in their pets for you to see. You may hold them or pet them if you like. They are all well behaved."

"They have germs!" Mrs. Crabtree shouted.

"The children will come around with their pets," said Marla. "You don't have to touch them if you don't want to. But these are house pets, and they are clean and cared for."

"Don't let them come near me," said Mrs. Crabtree in a cranky voice.

"Okay, children, you may circulate with your pets. You can skip Mrs. Crabtree."

That was a relief. Robert didn't want to go near her anyway.

Robert was on the other end of the lounge with Mr. Steiner, on the leather couch. Huckleberry sat very still and let Mr. Steiner pet him. "Good boy," said Robert. In another moment, Huckleberry had slid to the floor and curled up on Mr. Steiner's feet.

Over by the window, Susanne Lee was placing Fluffy in Mrs. Levine's arms. Mrs. Levine was smiling and petting the soft fur. Fluffy seemed to be enjoying it.

Two old women were reaching into the shoe box to pet Sunflower, Brian's guinea pig.

Robert let Huckleberry stay with Mr. Steiner while he showed Fuzzy to Mrs. Santini.

"Ooooh," said Mrs. Santini. "She's big, isn't she?" She didn't seem to be afraid. "And look at those hairy legs!"

All of a sudden, there was a commotion. "Biscuit! Come back!" Vanessa was crying. Somehow, the canary's cage door had opened, and the bird had escaped. He flew around the lounge, dipping and darting.

"Aieeeee!" squawked Mrs. Crabtree. "Get it out of here! It's going to get in my hair!" Marla ran over to Mrs. Crabtree.

Robert stared. Mrs. Crabtree hardly had any hair.

"Oh, for heaven's sake, Grace," said Mrs. Santini. "It's a little bird. Keep your shirt on."

Marla smiled and hid her mouth with her hand.

Biscuit landed on a curtain rod over the window. Fluffy jumped down from Mrs. Levine's lap and walked slowly toward the window. Uh-oh.

Robert quickly reached for an empty chair. "May I borrow this?" he asked Marla.

"Yes, sure. Take it."

Robert put the chair by the window. He climbed up slowly and carefully, trying not to scare the bird. Biscuit looked around.

Robert talked to Biscuit softly. "Hello, little bird," he said. "You just stay there now. . . ."

Susanne Lee tiptoed up to Fluffy and scooped her up.

Robert kept on talking as he figured out

what to do. Very slowly, he lifted his hand in front of the canary. He put out one finger. The bird watched his hand.

Robert moved his finger a tiny bit closer to the bird. He barely touched the bird's breast. The canary hopped onto Robert's finger. Still talking softly to her, Robert lowered the bird gently.

Vanessa had the cage waiting beside the chair Robert was standing on. Robert bent down and placed his finger right by

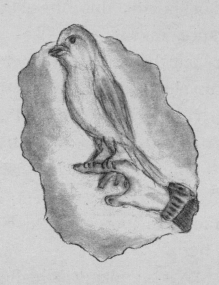

the cage door. Biscuit hopped inside. Vanessa shut the little door.

"Hurray for Robert!" said Marla. Everyone clapped, except for Mrs. Crabtree. She just sat with her lips pressed tightly together.

"I'd better go get Huckleberry," said Robert. When he came back, Mrs. Santini was laughing, holding Fuzzy's plastic tank up in front of Mrs. Crabtree.

"Get that thing away from me!" the cranky woman yelled, waving her bony hands to shoo it from her.

Mrs. Bernthal was apologizing to Marla when the director of the nursing home came into the lounge.

Marla greeted him. "Hello, Mr. Strauss."

"Hello, Ms. Edmonds," he said. "I hear there's been a bit of excitement here with Pet Day."

Marla smiled weakly. She had a feather on her skirt. Most of her hair had come undone.

"I always thought we could use more activity here in the afternoons," Mr. Strauss continued. "Maybe we should institute this as a regular thing."

Marla slumped into a chair. Mrs. Bernthal and the children laughed. So did many of the old people. Mrs. Crabtree still had not opened her mouth.

On the way home in the bus, Robert told Paul, "Old people are just like us. There are some bossy ones and some nice ones and some who are afraid of everything, and they even play tricks on each other." Like Charlie. Hmm. Maybe Charlie thought Robert was like Mrs. Crabtree. He sure had to think about that.

# The Wedding

The day of the wedding, Robert polished his good shoes. He put on a clean blue shirt, his new suit, and his watch and asked his mom to tie his tie.

As she wrapped one end of the tie around the other and pulled it together, she smiled. "You are incredibly handsome, Rob," she said. Mothers probably had to say that to their kids, but Robert liked hearing it anyway.

He sprayed his hair with stuff that Charlie used and had to admit he looked, and smelled, pretty good. Charlie even whistled a "guy" kind of whistle at him when he walked by.

The wedding was about half an hour's drive from River Edge. Robert rehearsed dance steps in his head, hoping he would remember where to put his feet.

At the synagogue, Robert, Charlie, and their dad were handed white yarmulkes, little skull caps. All the men wore them, even the groom. Up in front there was a canopy draped over four tall columns.

"That's the huppah," said Robert's dad. "The couple gets married under that."

The wedding was kind of long, but Robert amused himself. First, he counted the kids. Seven. Mostly teenagers or little kids.

Then he looked at the grown-ups. All the men wore suits and ties and had little white yarmulkes on their heads. Robert reached up and felt the one on his head.

He must look just like those men, only shorter. The women reminded Robert of a TV special he had seen on tropical birds. They wore bright colors—royal blue, emerald green, yellow—like jungle parrots. One even had sleeves that looked like wings. His own mother looked like a flamingo in her pink dress.

The bridal party was all dressed up, the women in matching pale blue gowns and the men in tuxedos. Three bridesmaids and three ushers slowly walked up the aisle, followed by a girl around Robert's age, carrying a basket. She had blond hair as curly as Robert's. She dropped rose petals from her basket onto the floor.

Cousin Heather was the last to walk down the aisle. She was dressed all in white with a veil over her head. Her father, Robert's Uncle Stanley, walked with her, his arm in hers.

Under the huppah, the rabbi said some prayers with the bride and groom.

"They're going to break a glass now," Charlie whispered to Robert.

"Who?" said Robert.

"The rabbi."

"Why?"

"I don't know. That's what he does. It's the custom," answered Charlie.

Robert could never be sure whether or not Charlie was teasing him. He kept watching the rabbi. The rabbi turned to the people and spoke. "If anyone knows of a reason why these two people, Heather and David, should not be married, let them speak now or forever hold their peace."

There wasn't a sound in the synagogue. Then—*beep beep! beep beep!*—a piercing sound filled the silence and everyone turned to look at Robert. Oh, no! His watch again! Robert jumped up and ran outside.

After he got the watch quiet again, he couldn't bring himself to go back inside. He wanted to see if the rabbi really broke a glass, like Charlie said he did, but what if his watch went off again?

He found a lounge area and sat down to wait until the wedding was over. He waited so long he went to the bathroom twice and had two paper cups of water at the water cooler. Finally, the music played and the doors opened, and Heather and David came out, followed by the crowd of people, all throwing birdseed. A photographer took pictures as they went down the stairs into a waiting limousine.

As the girl with the curly hair came out and saw him, she smiled. "See you later," she said. Robert watched her get into a limousine with others from the wedding party.

It looked like the rest of the day might be a little more interesting than the wedding part.

# Lindsey

The first good thing Robert discovered at the reception was that you didn't have to dance if you didn't want to. The band played fast music, even some rock and roll, so the fox trot and the waltz wouldn't work anyway.

Robert looked around and found the flower girl. She was up at the head banquet table with the rest of the wedding party. He was a couple of tables down with his parents and Charlie and several relatives he hardly knew.

"Psst!" Robert looked around. The girl was motioning him to come up to the banquet table. He turned to his mom.

"Is it okay, Mom?"

She smiled. "Sure. Go ahead."

YES! Robert jumped up and raced across the wooden floor, skidding to a stop next to the banquet table.

"Hi. Come on around," she said. "My name is Lindsey Ilana. What's yours?"

"Robert," said Robert, walking around to Lindsey's side of the table.

Robert sat in an empty chair. The bride and groom and several bridesmaids and their partners were dancing. The rest were sitting at the table, drinking wine and talking.

Lindsey plucked a grape from a fruit bowl and rolled it down the table. Robert grabbed it as it rolled by and popped it in his mouth. Lindsey laughed. Another grape came his way. Robert got that one, too.

As they continued to roll grapes, one of the bridesmaids and an usher came back to the table. A little later, more couples returned. Robert had to give up his chair.

"We can take a walk," said Lindsey, getting up.

Just as they were leaving, one of the bridesmaids cried out, "Oh! My earring!" She clutched at one ear that was empty. "I lost my earring."

"Maybe it's on the floor," said her partner. He bent over to look under the table.

"I'll get it," said Robert. He dove under the banquet table, glad to have a reason to do it. If he was younger, and not so dressed up, he probably would have spent the whole time there.

"I'll help," said Lindsey, crawling under the table with Robert.

On their hands and knees, Robert and Lindsey searched the floor. She went one way, and he went the other.

Finally, by the table leg, he saw something sparkly. It was the earring.

"I got it!" he shouted.

As they crawled back past all the feet, Lindsey giggled.

"What's so funny?" Robert asked.

"Look!" she said, pointing. The bridesmaids had slipped off their shoes and were in their stocking feet. In front of each pair of feet was a pair of shoes. They were all alike.

Robert looked at Lindsey and covered his mouth to keep from laughing out loud. Did she get the idea first or did he? Before he knew it, they had quickly rearranged the shoes so that nobody had the right pair near them.

They came out from under the table
and returned the earring to the bridesmaid. Everyone made a big fuss, especially
the bridesmaid with one earring.

"Thank you!" she said. "You guys are
the best!"

Robert knew if Lindsey giggled, he would burst out laughing, so he said, "That's okay," and ran for the back of the hall. Giggling, they watched until one of the bridesmaids got up and tried to slip on her shoes. She said something and another bridesmaid got up. There was confusion and giggling at the banquet table as bridesmaids tried to sort out the shoes. The ushers tried to help, but it got funnier as each bridesmaid kept trying on different shoes until she found the ones that fit.

Robert and Lindsey were laughing so hard Robert had to hold his stomach. Suddenly, he heard a voice behind him.

"What's so funny?" It was Charlie.

"Charlie!" said Robert, staring at his brother. He swallowed hard. At first, he was going to say, "Nothing." Then he looked at Lindsey, who was still laughing. And he looked over at the banquet table. It was too good to resist. He told Charlie what they had done.

A big grin spread over Charlie's face. "You did that?" he asked.

Robert nodded.

"Cool!" said his brother.

*What do you know*, thought Robert. *I just impressed my brother.*

# Prince Charming

**W**atching from the banquet table as the others danced, Robert looked at his watch. It was blinking, but he had no idea why. He shook his wrist.

"I have the world's worst wristwatch," he told Lindsey. "It goes off when I don't want it to, and now it's started blinking, and I don't know why.

"Let me look at it," said Lindsey. Robert took off the watch and handed it to her.

"Maybe it's broken," he said.

Lindsey played around with the watch for a while and gave it back to him. "It's not broken," she said. "It won't go off again unless you set the alarm."

"What did you do?" he asked.

"I pressed in these two buttons here. That shut off the alarm."

"Great," said Robert. "Thanks." How did she know that? Did girls know everything?

"So why was it blinking?" asked Robert, strapping the watch onto his wrist again.

"Someone must have set it to do that as a reminder of something. I reset it—for 8:32 pm—that's right now. When you see it blink next time, you can remember this exact moment, wherever you are and what-ever you're doing. Just press the buttons like I showed you to shut it off, if you want."

"No, I like it. I won't shut it off."

Lindsey smiled.

"Ladies and gentlemen," announced the deejay. "This is the final round of dances. We'll be playing a few slow songs as we wind down. When we're ready for our final number, we'll give you a warning, so you can find that someone special to dance it with.

Robert was gazing into space when the music began again. As soon as he heard it, he knew.

"Lindsey, will you dance with me?" he asked.

"I don't know how," she said. He smiled. Maybe girls didn't know everything.

"I can teach you," he said. They went out on the dance floor. Robert showed Lindsey the one, two, three, four pattern. It worked fine, even without footprints to follow.

The next song was a little different.

Robert felt the one, two, three rhythm. "Wow. I can do this, too!" Robert said.

"You can?" Lindsey looked totally surprised.

"Yeah. Look." He showed Lindsey how to circle, taking one step on each beat— one, two, three, one, two, three. Lindsey was a good learner. She picked it up fast.

As the waltz ended, the deejay announced the very last dance of the evening. "I . . . I'm sorry, but I have to go," said Robert. "I have to do something."

"Okay," said Lindsey. She looked a little puzzled as she sat down, but Robert knew she would understand.

He felt very handsome in his new suit and very grown up as he asked his mom for the last dance.